This Little Tiger book belongs to:

 St Robert Southwell Catholic Primary School

Welcome to Reception 2022
A gift to you from the
Governors Charitable Foundation

In memory of Mary Upshaw Broach and for my
first grandchild, Kai Gray McGee, a very happy boy! ~ M M

For Freya – always say "boo" to a goose! ~ A E

LITTLE TIGER PRESS LTD,
an imprint of the Little Tiger Group
1 Coda Studios, 189 Munster Road, London SW6 6AW
Imported into the EEA by Penguin Random House Ireland,
Morrison Chambers, 32 Nassau Street, Dublin D02 YH68
www.littletiger.co.uk

First published in Great Britain 2008
This edition published 2016

A CIP catalogue record for this book is available from the British Library

Printed in China • LTP/2700/4238/1121

2 4 6 8 10 9 7 5 3

Silly Goose

Marni McGee

Alison Edgson

LiTTLE TiGER

LONDON

Goose was very happy. Sun was shining. Bird was singing. Bee was buzzing in the flowers. Goose began to dance on the banks of Frog Jump Pond.

Goose saw Fox. "Good morning, Fox," she called.

But Fox didn't say, "Good morning." Instead he said, "Goose, your ears are missing."

"My ears?" Goose
gasped. "Missing?"
Fox held out
his paws. "Look
in the pond. What
do you see?"

Goose looked. "I see
my white feathers, my
long-long neck and my beautiful wings."
  "Ah," said Fox, "but do you see your ears?"
  "Well no," said Goose, "but I can fix that, dear Fox."
And she set two pink flowers on her head.

"Pahhh," scoffed Fox. "Ears are not soft
and pink. Ears are stiff, pointy things – with fur."
"Where could my ears be?" wondered Goose.
"Did you take them off?" asked Fox.
"Must have," said Goose. "I guess . . .
May I have *your* ears, dear Fox?"

"No," snapped Fox. "You may not.
They're the wrong colour for you."
  "Oh dear," said Goose. And
off she ran until she
met Rabbit.

"Rabbit," said Goose. "I have lost my ears somewhere, somehow. May I have *your* ears, dear Rabbit?"

"No, silly Goose," sighed Rabbit. "They would be too long for you."

"Oh dear," said Goose, and off she ran until she met Cow.

"Cow," cried Goose,
"I have lost my ears! I must,
 I *must* have ears right now.
 May I have *your* ears, dear Cow?"
   "Such a silly Goose!" Cow grumbled.
"My ears would be too big for you."

"Oh dear, oh dear," wailed Goose.
But just then she heard someone calling:

"Ears for sale!
Get your ears from Peacock's shop!"

Goose saw a
strange bird with
bright feathers, bows
and trailing ribbons.

"I would like two white ears,
if you please," she said.
    Peacock bowed low. "Come to
my shop, madam," he said. "We will
choose the perfect ears for a delicious –
I mean, *delightful* – creature like you."
    "Goodie," gushed Goose, and off they pranced.
    Goose did not notice his pointy snout,
his sharp teeth, or his bushy red tail.

But Rabbit saw. "Peacocks do *not* have pointy snouts, sharp teeth, or bushy red tails," he thought. His whiskers trembled with the truth: "Peacock is Fox in disguise!" Quickly he gathered the animals.

"Hurry-hurry-hurry," he cried.

"Fox has tricked our poor, silly Goose."

So the animals trotted, hopped,

and flew to save Goose.

Meanwhile Goose and Fox had reached his den.
"Stand near the fire, Goose," he commanded.
"I shall choose the perfect ears for you."

As she waited, Goose began to *think*. "I *hear* that crackling fire, and I *heard* what Peacock said just now." "Peacock," she exclaimed. "I can hear!" "Pahhh," he scoffed. "You're imagining things."

Just then the animals arrived at Fox's den.

"Goose," called Rabbit, "are you there?"

"We have come," buzzed Bee.

"Are you there? Are you there?"

Goose flapped her wings with delight.
"Peacock, I hear my friends. I do not need
new ears. I have my ears . . . somewhere.
I *am* a silly goose, I guess.
And now I must be going.
Goodbye, dear Peacock.
Bye-bye."

"Ooooooooh, no," Fox sneered and bolted
the door. "You are not going *anywhere*, Goose."
He flung off his cloak, his ribbons and bows.

"*Fox!*" gasped Goose.

"Yes," said Fox. "It is I – Fox. And I am
going to eat you, Goose."

"Oh dear, oh DEAR," cried Goose.
"I am done-for, finished, COOKED!"

Just then, Bird pecked a hole in the wall
– big enough for Bee. Bee zoomed in
and stung Fox on the nose. Fox howled.
Goose honked with excitement.

With a flick of her wings, she snatched
Fox's cloak. She slung it over his head
and tied him up.

And then with one mighty kick,
Cow broke down the door.

Fox wriggled free and ran,
but the animals ran after him.
With Goose in the lead, they chased
that wicked Fox far, far away . . .

Fox was never, ever seen again.

And Goose was very, very happy!